# The Story of King Lion

First published in 1912 in German under the title
*König Löwes Hochzeitsschmaus*
This edition published by Floris Books in 2013

English version © Floris Books 2013

British Library CIP Data available
ISBN 978-086315-949-7
Printed in Malaysia

# The Story of
# King Lion

### Sibylle von Olfers

## Floris Books

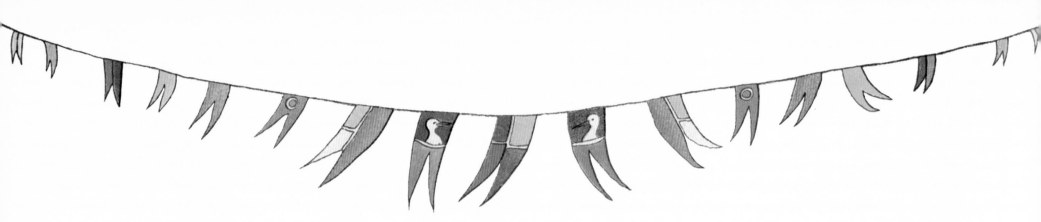

"I shall have a great feast,"
said the King of the Beasts.
"Everyone must bring
their favourite treat.

The creature whose offering
pleases me best,
shall help me in future
rule over the rest."

Each animal wanted
the praise of the King,
so they rushed off to cook,
squibble-squabbling.

King Lion sat back.
He'd not long to wait,
before Stork carried in
frog pâté on a plate.

The pig returned next,
and he looked very proud.
"I've made truffle stew,"
he grunted out loud.

STORK

PIG

The donkey thinks prickly
thistles are delicious.
He mixed up a salad
both spiky and nutritious.

"What shall I bring?"
Bear quietly said.
The bees had the answer:
a sweet honey bread.

DONKEY

BEAR

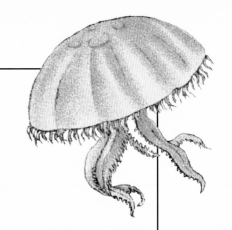

The shimmering fish
proudly displayed
her tastiest, fizziest
saltwater lemonade.

Seal knew exactly
what the King would like,
"Nothing could be better
than horseradish and pike!"

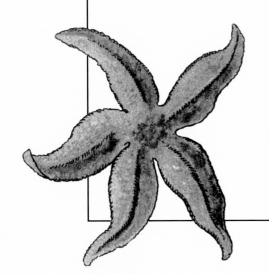

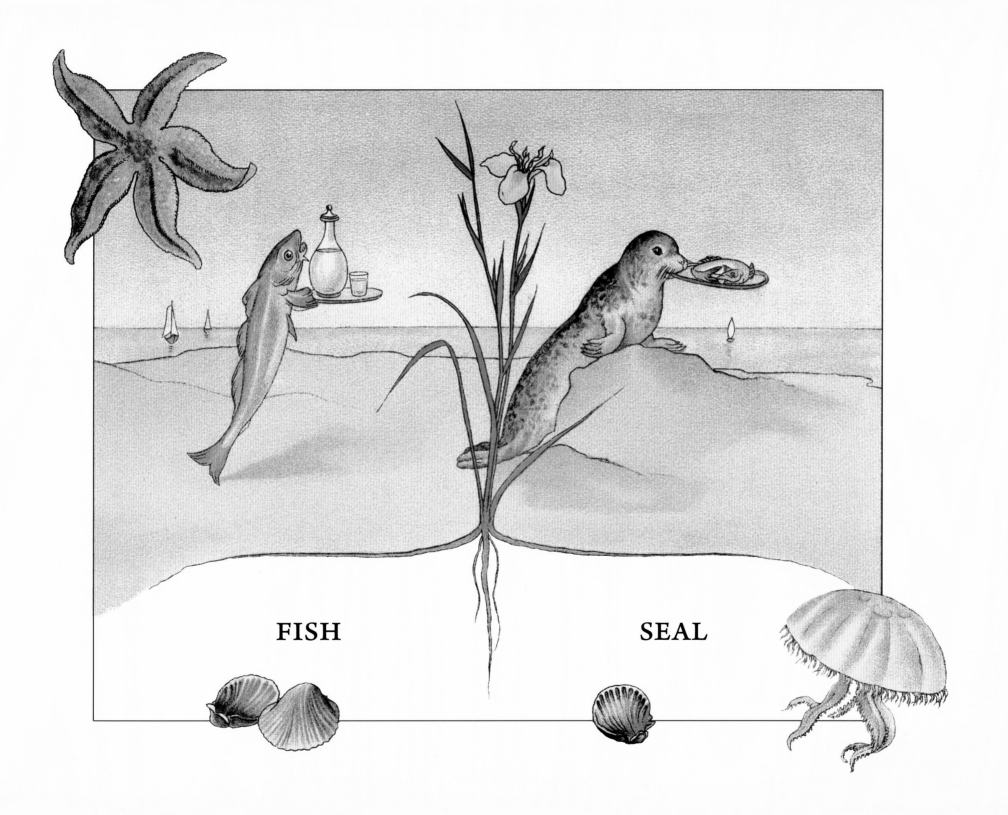

FISH                    SEAL

The plump red cherries
that Sparrow loves to steal
made a thick fruity jam:
her favourite meal.

Juicy old bones
boiled up in a crock
and stirred by the Dog
gave a sumptuous stock.

SPARROW                 DOG

Hen brought fresh eggs,
as only she can,
cooked to perfection
in her iron frying pan.

The cow made a cheesecake
a real dairy dream,
and to eat alongside it,
a bowl full of cream.

HEN                    COW

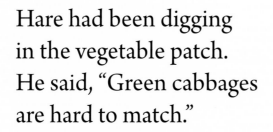

Hare had been digging
in the vegetable patch.
He said, "Green cabbages
are hard to match."

Fox was sure
he would outdo the rest,
"Isn't roast goose
what we all love best?"

HARE
FOX

Hedgehog has a recipe
that never fails.
He made his sausages
out of snails!

Rabbit said, "This contest
will soon be over
when the King tastes my soup
made from carrots and clover."

**HEDGEHOG**

**RABBIT**

Beetles and bugs
arranged in a bowl
made a crunchy snack,
enjoyed by Mole.

"It's perfect for breakfast,
and tea, and for lunch,"
said Butterfly, sipping her
sweet nectar punch.

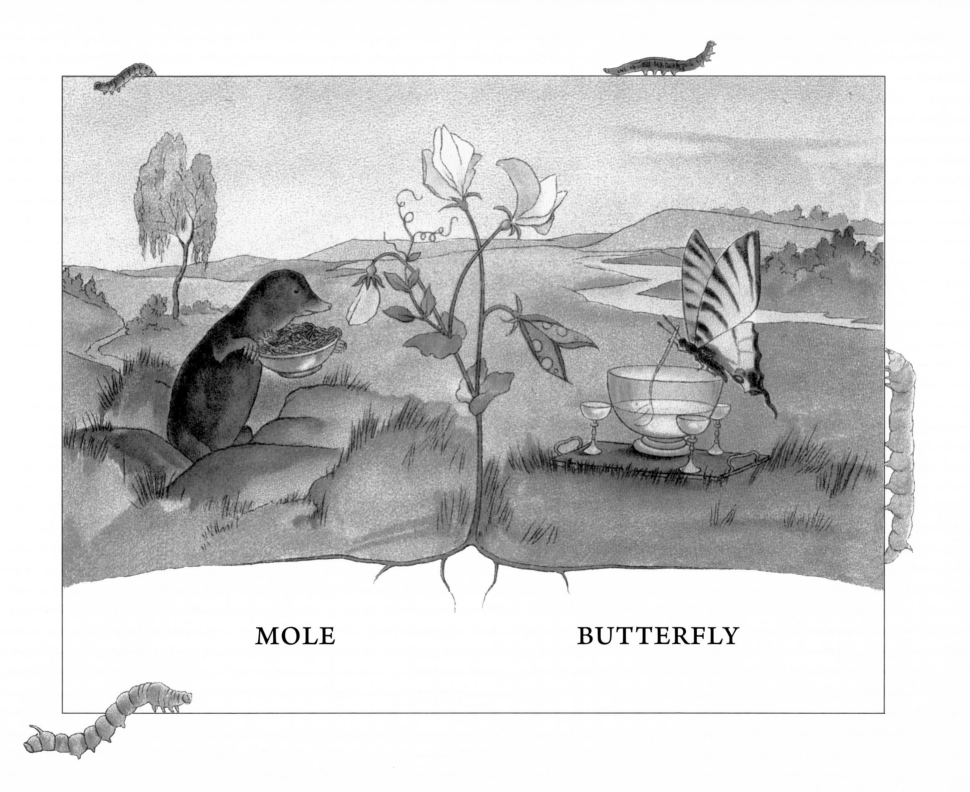

MOLE                                    BUTTERFLY

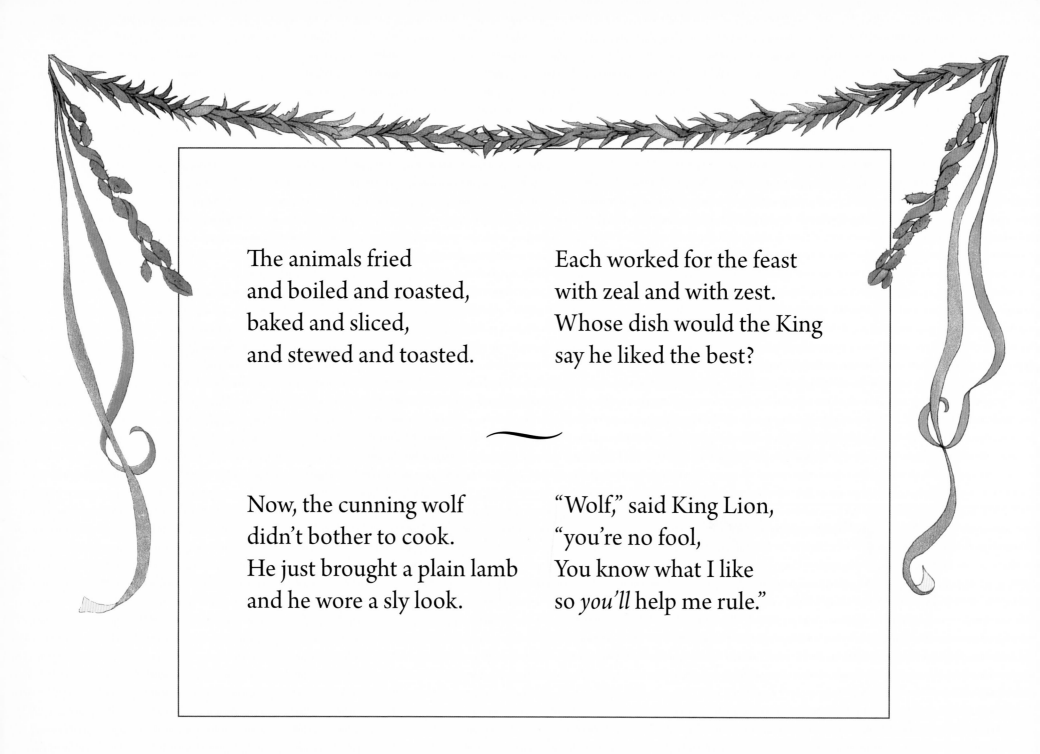

The animals fried
and boiled and roasted,
baked and sliced,
and stewed and toasted.

Each worked for the feast
with zeal and with zest.
Whose dish would the King
say he liked the best?

Now, the cunning wolf
didn't bother to cook.
He just brought a plain lamb
and he wore a sly look.

"Wolf," said King Lion,
"you're no fool,
You know what I like
so *you'll* help me rule."

WOLF                    LION

# Sibylle von Olfers

Sibylle von Olfers' (1881–1916) blend of natural obser-
vation and simple design has led to comparisons with
Kate Greenaway and Elsa Beskow.

She was born the third of five children in a castle in
East Prussia. Encouraged by her aunt, she trained at art
college. Her beauty attracted many admirers and suitors,
but she remained aloof and distant from the "useless world
of the aristocrats".

At the age of twenty-five she joined the Sisters of
Saint Elisabeth, an order of nuns. As well as teaching art
in the local school, she wrote and illustrated a number of
children's books. Tragically, she died at the age of thirty-
four from a lung infection.

*The Story of the Snow Children* is Olfers' first book, published in 1905. Her other books include *The Story of the Root Children* (1906), *The Story of the Rabbit Children* (1906), *The Story of Little Billy Bluesocks* (1906), *The Princess in the Forest* (1909), *The Story of the Wind Children* (1910) and *The Story of the Butterfly Children* (1916).

   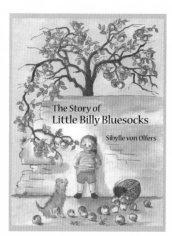